ALSO BY ANDREW CLEMENTS

Big Al

Frindle

The Landry News

The Janitor's Boy

The School Story

BIG AL and Shrimpy

Andrew Clements

Yoshi

SIMON & SCHUSTER BOOKS FOR YOUNG READERS
New York London Toronto Sydney Singapore

Thanks to Thomas Smith, director of Environmental Education at the Berkshire Museum.

SIMON & SCHUSTER BOOKS FOR YOUNG READERS
An imprint of Simon & Schuster Children's Publishing Division
1230 Avenue of the Americas, New York, New York 10020

Book design by Paula Winicur
The text for this book is set in Centaur.
Printed in Hong Kong
2 4 6 8 10 9 7 5 3 1

Library of Congress Cataloging-in-Publication Data
Clements, Andrew, 1949-
Big Al and Shrimpy / by Andrew Clements; illustrated by Yoshi.
p.   cm.
Summary: Shrimpy learns that even though he may be small, he can still make a big difference to his friend, Big Al.

ISBN 0-689-84247-3
[1. Size—Fiction. 2. Friendship—Fiction. 3. Fishes—Fiction.] I. Yoshi, ill. II. Title
PZ7.C59118 Bj 2002
[E]—dc21   2001031305

For my sisters, Martha and Frances —A .C.

To my children, Hibiki and Miki —Y.

In the wide blue sea there was a very clever fish named Shrimpy.
You could not find a smarter fish.

But Shrimpy was also very,

very

small.

Shrimpy wanted to be like Big Al, but no one wanted
to be friends with a tiny fish like him.

So Shrimpy was lonely, and he cried little
salty tears into the big salty sea.

One day all the fish said, "Let's play tag!"
Big Al said, "Me too!"
And Shrimpy said, "Yeah, me too!"

When the game started, Big Al was it. Big Al was fast, but he couldn't zigzag. He couldn't tag anyone except for Shrimpy.

Then Shrimpy was it. Shrimpy was too slow. He couldn't catch anyone.

But Shrimpy was smart.

He waited in just the right place, and then he tagged Big Al.

All the other fish said, "No fair!

Shrimpy and Big Al are just tagging each other!"

So Big Al and Shrimpy had to leave the game.

And that's when Big Al and Shrimpy became best friends.

For Shrimpy, it was great to have a big, strong friend.
Shrimpy could fly through the water, faster than ever before.

Shrimpy always had plenty to eat.

And Shrimpy went new places with Big Al.

One day Shrimpy and Big Al went to the edge of the Big Deep.

Shrimpy had never seen the Big Deep before. The Big Deep was too scary.

But not now. With Big Al next to him,
Shrimpy felt just fine.

They went right up to the edge and looked over.
It was dark in there.
The Big Deep went down

and down

and down.

It went down so far that some fish
said there was no bottom at all.

Shrimpy said, "Could you push a rock down there?"

Big Al puffed himself up and said, "Sure I could. Just watch."

Big Al pushed a round green rock.

He flipped his tail and he flapped his fins.

The rock moved a little, and then it went over the edge.

Big Al and Shrimpy listened.

The rock tumbled down and down and down.

Then all was quiet again.
Shrimpy said, "That was great!"
Big Al smiled and puffed himself up.
He said, "Watch this! I'll push another one—even bigger!"

Big Al pushed on a huge white rock.
He flipped his tail and he flapped his fins.
The rock moved a little, and Big Al pushed harder.
Then over the edge it went, but Big Al said,

"Oh no! Hellllp!"

His fin was stuck in a crack on the rock!
The rock went tumbling down into the Big Deep,
and Big Al went with it.

Shrimpy was scared.
He swam back to get all the other fish.
"Come quick! We have to help Big Al!"

All the fish came to the edge of the Big Deep.
One fish said, "We can't go down there.
It's too deep and dark."
Everyone was ready to give up.

But not Shrimpy.
He said, "We have to help Big Al—and I know how!"

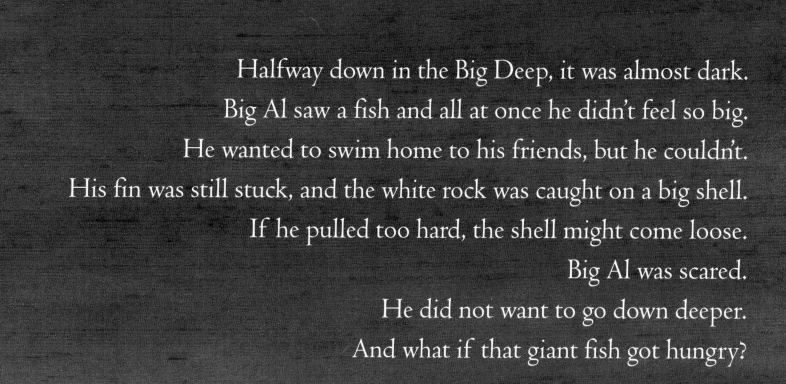

Halfway down in the Big Deep, it was almost dark.
Big Al saw a fish and all at once he didn't feel so big.
He wanted to swim home to his friends, but he couldn't.
His fin was still stuck, and the white rock was caught on a big shell.
If he pulled too hard, the shell might come loose.
Big Al was scared.
He did not want to go down deeper.
And what if that giant fish got hungry?

Suddenly, just above him, Big Al saw a light.
The giant fish saw it too, and he swam away fast.

The light came closer and closer.

It was a lantern fish—and Shrimpy!

Shrimpy looked at the rock,

and he looked at the shell,

and he looked at Big Al's fin.

Then Shrimpy gave some orders.

Ten little fish held the shell,
and ten little fish held the white rock.
Then Shrimpy and ten other little fish
   pulled on Big Al's fin.

Pop! It came loose—and just in time.

The white rock wobbled,
and then it tumbled down
to the deepest part of the Big Deep.

Then Shrimpy told everyone to turn around.

The chain of fish swam up and up and up, and Big Al followed Shrimpy, headed for home.

There was a party that night.
Everyone was happy that Big Al was safe.
But the guest of honor was Shrimpy,
the little fish with the big ideas.